CROSSING THE STREAMS

Book Four of *Revin's Heart*

STEVEN D. BREWER

Published by Water Dragon Publishing
waterdragonpublishing.com

An imprint of Paper Angel Press
paperangelpress.com

ISBN 978-1-957146-77-5 (Trade Paperback)

FIRST EDITION

10 9 8 7 6 5 4 3 2 1

AUTHOR'S NOTE

In 2007, on its fiftieth anniversary, I read *On the Road* by Jack Kerouac. It made a big impact on me, although I'm sure it resonated more with people of my parents' generation. But as I was writing this part, I realized that this installment is Revin's *On the Road*.

Revin learns a lot about the places he's going through. And, as usual, he learns a lot about himself as well. He's starting to understand that his choices impact the people around him. And that his acceptance of things as they are reinforces and strengthens them. We also learn a lot more about the enigmatic Professor. And we meet some new characters who will have profound influences on Revin's life.

Finally, we also gain insight into the overall political system within which these island fiefdoms operate. We haven't heard much about this before — not because it isn't important, but because of Revin's lack of experience with any of this. Revin is an autodidact; he basically had no access to schooling while growing up. He's learned a lot since, but there's still a lot he doesn't know. And there's a lot more he's going to have to learn.

CROSSING THE STREAMS

T HE *QUEEN OF BELLERIAND* slipped almost silently through the tranquil night air. The timekeeper quietly struck second bell. Revin heard muffled thumps as the shift changed and new men came on duty while others retired to their hammocks. Most of the pirates were already asleep, but Revin was too keyed up after the day's events. In his mind's eye, he kept seeing the man's face as he was run through ... No. When Revin ran his sword through him. He'd had the shakes off and on for a while and so, to distract himself, he started to read Momo's diary.

He smiled at her descriptions of things that seemed ordinary to her, but were almost unbelievable to him: traveling to the country house by carriage, attending a costume holiday ball, a full day spent shopping for shoes ... The scenes implied by these activities were nearly beyond his comprehension. Then there were her dreams and aspirations that were sprinkled liberally throughout. Although she did not name him explicitly among them, Revin wondered if he was not reading between the lines that she imagined them together.

Revin read the final entry in Momo's journal, then snuffed out the lantern and sat with his head in his hands. He was becoming more and more confused about his own feelings. "Temper your expectations," the Baron had told him. What were those, exactly? He closed his eyes and tried to still his unquiet heart.

The next morning, the *Queen* returned to her berth on the steep side of Kapper Island, where the pirate's secret base was located. The men who'd been on duty went to sleep, but Will called Grip, Revin, and the Professor in for a strategy meeting.

When Revin arrived, he saw that there was an unfamiliar face there as well — a wizened, older man with thin white hair and reading spectacles. He was looking through a ledger, making notations with a pencil. He looked up as Revin came in.

"Revin," Will said. "I'd like you to meet Mr. Brill, our bursar."

"How do you do," Revin said, resisting the urge to curtsy.

Brill looked at him over his glasses and then nodded curtly.

Revin felt slightly nonplussed at the non-verbal answer, but didn't think too much about it. When Grip and the Professor arrived, Will called the meeting to order.

"Gentleman," Will said. "We have been informed of a serious threat to our operations. Havelock is developing an Etheric Storm Generator that can leave us dead in the water in the vicinity of a large storm. We will investigate this threat.

"As some of you already know, we have received a — let's call it a 'donation' — to subsidize our operations. Two hundred reggies. But ..." At this point, Will looked around the table locking eyes with each man in turn. "We are not being paid to do this work. These funds will be expended only in support of this operation. That means that any expense will need to be justified to Mr. Brill who will hold the funds and disburse them only under those circumstances.

"Do you have anything to add, Mr. Brill?" Will concluded.

Brill shook his head.

"Who is going to go, then?" asked Revin.

"Ah! You bring up a good point, lad," Will said. "First of all, I think we can all agree that the Professor should go to help ensure we collect the right information to understand the device."

There were murmurs of assent from everyone present, except Mr. Brill, who was silent.

"I understand that, after my last little visit," Will continued. "I am *persona non grata* in Havelock."

"There were Wanted posters on the last packet ship we took with five hundred reggies for you. And not a bad likeness either," Grip said. "They're only offering one hundred for me." He scowled as if his personal worth were up for question.

"That's right," Will said. "But Revin here was wearing a disguise."

Revin blushed, remembering how Will had convinced him to pass for a prostitute by wearing a dress and pink wig.

"So I propose that Revin and the Professor should go," Will concluded.

"Well, you'll not have me traipsing all over the countryside," the Professor thundered, pounding his fist on the table. "I'm not riding in some wagon either. If I'm to go, we're getting a coach. A nice one. And that's a legitimate expense," he said, glaring at Mr. Brill.

Brill looked up briefly, nodded, and returned to his ledger.

"What should be the plan for once we get there?" Revin asked.

"That's your business," the Professor grumbled. "You're the leader of this little adventure. I'm just going to see this device."

"Maybe you can talk to the Duke's seneschal," Will asked. "Maybe you can still talk him into giving you a job!"

"How do I explain where I've been for the past few months?"

"I'm sure you'll think of something," Will laughed.

Revin was not reassured.

"And how are we even going to get back?" Revin asked.

"Here, Lad," Will said. "Here's a map of Havelock I found. I don't know how useful it will be because it's but a tourist map. Still, it's better than naught. See this place on the west coast?"

"Beskin Harbor?" Revin asked.

"Yes. It looks like a quiet little fishing village," Will continued. "Since the harbor is too small for anything larger than fishing boats. There's nothing there, so there shouldn't be many patrols. The *Queen* will begin to stand off-and-on every day for the hour before sunset — that should give you good light to signal with."

•   •   •

The next morning, just before dawn, the *Queen* dropped Revin and the Professor in a small dinghy off the coast near Beskin Harbor. Revin started rowing and, once again, thanked his training that had helped him recover so quickly from his ordeal in Belleriand. *And Momo,* he thought, remembering her in the bath with him. He was glad he was sitting with his back to the Professor while he rowed, so he couldn't see Revin's face.

"When we get ashore, how should I introduce you?" Revin said.

"Why don't we just say I'm your uncle," the Professor said. "That's vague and irrefutable."

"Ok ... Uncle," Revin said.

The waves were light in the pre-dawn and they made good time. Revin was able to row right up to the shore in town and pull the boat up onto the cobblestone beach. The Professor jumped out and struggled through the cobbles, hand walking with his arm braces. Revin pulled the boat above the high-water mark where a whole line of other small boats were stowed. Then, after grabbing their bags, he flipped it over.

They walked along the harbor to the road that ran up to the pier, where they saw several larger water craft tied up. Then they turned inland and followed the road under a low archway into a promenade that had small cafes, eateries, and other touristy businesses. Most were still closed, but one cafe was open.

Revin left the Professor in the cafe to get breakfast while he scouted around for transportation. About twenty minutes later, he returned and ordered some breakfast for himself.

"I couldn't find a coach for hire here," Revin said. "They said we'll probably have better luck in the capital. But there is a coach leaving for the capital in an hour and I've booked us seats."

"Good enough," the Professor replied. "The breakfast here is great. Be sure to try the preserves! They're homemade!"

•   •   •

Revin stepped off the coach in Havelock and held the door for the Professor, who hopped down with his arm braces. Revin had slept a good part of the way, but had also spent several hours studying the map, selecting locations, and concocting a story about them to explain his absence. He hoped.

Revin led the Professor back toward the University. Revin experienced a profound sense of *deja vu* returning to his familiar haunts. Revin walked up to the guards at the University gate trying to project an air of confidence.

"Do you remember me?" he asked.

"Um ... Oh! Just a minute!" one said. "You're Revin, right? You were with Professor Dirge. Where have you been?"

"Well, Dirge and I went for a research trip and he was taken ill. I stayed with him, but he kept getting sicker and finally passed away last week. So I'm back to figure out what to do next."

"You'll probably have to speak with the Provost," the man said. "He won't be in until tomorrow."

"Actually," said the other. "The Duke's seneschal came here, impounded your trunks, and secured your chambers after you didn't come back. You should probably skip the Provost and go speak directly with him."

Revin bowed and thanked the men. He stood conferring with the Professor about what to do for the night when someone said, "Professor Grexin? Is that you?"

"Eh?" the Professor said, turning toward the newcomer, a middle-aged academic wearing University garb.

"It is you!" the man continued excitedly. "You probably don't remember me: Niles Ender. I saw your talk five years ago on hydrogen generation using algae and we spoke for a bit at the reception that followed. What are you doing back here?"

"I'm just visiting my nephew," the Professor said, clapping Revin on the back.

"Wow! You must be so proud to have a famous uncle like Professor Grexin! Where are you staying?"

"Actually, we're about to look for lodging," Revin said. "Since our rooms are unavailable."

"Nonsense! We can put you up in our chambers. I'd love the chance to pick your uncle's brain! Come this way!"

•　　　•　　　•

The next morning, Revin left at first light and walked to the city center. He found the Executive Building where the government offices were located and, inside, located the office of the Seneschal. They were not open for another hour, so he went back out and found a nearby cafe to wait. He ordered a cup of coffee, and then spent the time carefully rehearsing his story.

They were opening the door just as he returned to the office.

"I'm Revin Minerson. I'm here to speak with the Seneschal," Revin announced to the receptionist.

"Do you have an appointment?" she inquired.

Revin shook his head.

"Take a seat and I'll see what I can do."

The Seneschal had a lavish set of offices adjacent to the Duke in the Executive Building. Dark wood paneling formed the basis of the décor, complemented by huge oil paintings depicting scenes of battle. A large collection of captured regimental battle flags hung from the ceiling. Revin spied one with Belthingstone colors.

Revin waited for more than an hour and grew increasingly anxious. He kept wondering if guards would appear to clap him in irons and drag him off. But he just sat quietly as others came and went. Finally, the receptionist motioned to him and he came to his feet.

"The Seneschal will see you now," she said.

Revin walked through the doorway into the Seneschal's office and then stood quietly while the Seneschal finished writing something and then looked up. Revin bowed deeply.

"Thank you very much for seeing me, sir," Revin began. "I very much appreciate you taking the time from your busy schedule."

"You've got balls to just walk in here," the Seneschal said. "Where in the ether have you been? You and Dirge just disappeared. And at a particularly suspicious point in time, I might point out. I thought about just calling the guards and letting them sort out this mess."

"Professor Dirge and I were on a research trip to the Hermitage to consult their library," Revin said. "He always had a fascination with the history of the law and there was a particular book he learned of that he wanted to consult."

"The Hermitage, eh?" the Seneschal said. "That makes sense, I guess. But why are you only coming back now?"

"On the way back," Revin continued. "Professor Dirge was taken ill at Sendia Springs."

"Well, if you're going to get ill, that's just as nice a place as any."

"We made it as far as Beskin Harbor when he took a turn for the worse. I've been there, taking care of him this whole time. But he kept getting sicker and sicker until he passed away two days ago."

"He's dead?"

"Yes, sir," Revin said. "Regrettably."

"What did he die of?" the Seneschal asked.

"The doctor said it was quinsy," Revin replied. "They tried everything they could think of, but it was no use."

"Quinsy, eh?"

"Quinsy, sir," Revin agreed.

"So you're here because you're now without a position. And you say you've just been to the Hermitage and Beskin Harbor?"

"Yes, sir. If you would be so kind, sir."

"When you both disappeared at nearly the same time as the attack on the admiralty," he said, grimacing, "There was some suspicion Dirge was involved: the description of one of the attackers sounded like it could have been him. The other wasn't you, though: It was some woman. A prostitute, by all reports."

"Thank you for your confidence, sir," Revin said.

The Seneschal paused for a moment in thought and then regarded Revin seriously.

"I'll tell you what," he said. "I need someone to run an errand. An important errand, mind you."

"I won't let you down, sir," Revin said. "You can count on me!"

"It's funny you mentioned those places. As it turns out, I need someone to escort a key scientist, who's been working on an important project, from the Hermitage to Beskin Harbor to complete his work."

"An important project, sir?"

"Yes. I'm sorry, but I can't tell you any more about it. It's top secret. But if you can take care of this errand for me, I'm sure we can find more for you to do."

"Understood. Thank you so much for this opportunity to prove myself, sir," Revin said. "You'll see whether or not I can be trusted."

"You'll need to hire a coach. Just a moment," he said, scrawling several notes on paper. "Give this note to my secretary. She'll get you a purse with 25 reggies. That should be enough to hire a coach — and a driver, if you need one. Give this other note to the Director at the Hermitage. He'll introduce you to the scientist. And be sure to show him a good time. Go ahead and stop at Sendia Springs on the way."

"You can count on me, sir," Revin said, accepting the pieces of paper. "Can I ask for one more thing, sir?"

Revin paused and the Seneschal gestured at him to continue.

"I understand that my and Professor Dirge's trunks were impounded by your office. Could those be released to me?"

"Certainly," the Seneschal said, writing a third note. "They were searched, of course, but nothing was found. Take this to the University."

After Revin collected the funds and departed the Seneschal's office, he went to the shop the office had recommended to hire a coach. The shop owner, Hirus Darkpony, a prosperous older man, showed Revin around an enclosure where they had a number of different coaches available for hire. They had a variety to choose from, and he ended up selecting a coach on the larger side which seated four comfortably and was drawn by a team of four horses.

"You know, then, how to manage horses and drive a team, Milord?" the shop owner asked.

"Well ... No. Not really, to be honest," Revin said. "Is there someone we could hire?"

"We have a list of coachmen for hire," Darkpony said. "But they're not affiliated with our shop. If you choose one from the list, we'll send a boy to get him, and he can bring the coach to you wherever you like."

"Hmm. I guess I'll just take this first one, Arthur Aaron," Revin said. "Have him bring the coach to the University at first light tomorrow."

"You'll need to pay him eight reggies," said Darkpony. "You should leave four as earnest money and pay him the rest when you get back."

Revin handed over 16 reggies for the coach, deposit and earnest money. He fingered one of the other coins and studied it. He'd seen other people with reggies before, but he'd never, himself, even held a gold coin. These were new, with crisp markings, showing the likeness of King Reginald the Arbiter who ruled on Harway over all of the island nations.

Returning to the University, Revin gave the slip of paper from the Seneschal to the guards. One of them took him to a storage room where he was able to recover the trunks.

After the dinner, he and the Professor shut themselves in their room to take a closer look inside them.

"Now watch this, Revin," the Professor said. "You said you didn't find anything inside Dirge's trunk. But you didn't know then that he was an agent. I think we should take a closer look at the trunk itself."

The Professor tapped along the trunk's edges, listening for changes in pitch. When he heard something, he began feeling carefully and found first one, and then two, rivets that could be pulled part way out. This released a long thin section of wood that could be persuaded to slide out. The slat had holes cut in it that each contained one of 25 reggies. A bit more exploring revealed a matching arrangement on the other side of the trunk that revealed 22 gold coins. He had evidently spent the others on their passage on the ill-fated *Madeline*.

"I suggest we put this money back where it was," the Professor said. "I'll start using this trunk. Let's try to use the Baron's money first and only use this in an emergency. Or if Brill tries to stiff us when we get back," he concluded with a devious chuckle.

At first light, Revin dragged their baggage out and was on hand when the coach arrived. The coachman, a tall, gangly man in his 20s, introduced himself, hat in hand, and then helped to load the trunks in the baggage compartment at the rear of the coach. Revin followed the Professor into the coach and they set off for the Hermitage.

They spent the morning rolling through an increasingly rural landscape. Unlike in Belleriand -- at least in the parts Revin had recently traversed, where the farms seemed like small land-holders -- here they seemed like giant agricultural enterprises, with gangs of laborers supervised by overseers. Revin found it chilling to watch the overseers menacing and bullying the workers, even as some of the workers collapsed in the heat.

By midafternoon, they had reached a vast expanse of arid grassland. Revin opened the window that communicated between the coach and the box where the driver sat.

"Hey, Art, how much farther do we intend to go today?"

"Well, Milord," Art said. "It's going to take most of the next day, so a bit more today will give us more flexibility tomorrow.

Revin closed the window and turned to the Professor.

"Why is everyone calling me 'milord'?" he wondered aloud.

"Heh," chuckled the Professor. "You're a handsome young man with a pocket full of gold. Of course, people are going to assume the worst."

Near sunset, they arrived at a large tree that stood alone in the grassland near the road. Art drew the horses to a stop and set the brake. While Revin pulled together a meal with supplies he'd brought, and the Professor busied himself with building a small fire, the coachman unhooked the horses, staked them out where they could graze, watered them, brushed them, and gave each a feedbag.

After dinner, while Art checked the horses and collected their feedbags, Revin and the Professor got ready to sleep. They were about to get into the bedrolls when Art appeared around the corner of the wagon accompanied by two other men. With their swords drawn, they charged toward Revin and the Professor.

Revin drew his sword and put himself *en garde*. Considering the Professor no threat, Art and the two men bypassed him to attack Revin. Revin began to panic, wondering how he could possibly defend himself against all three of them. Suddenly, the two other men staggered and, with their eyes rolling up in their heads, collapsed. Art looked surprised and distracted at the sudden loss of his allies. Revin lunged forward and caught him in the throat. Art fell over clutching at his neck and expired with blood spurting through his fingers.

Revin stared wild-eyed at the Professor, who stood with his arm braces raised.

"What just happened?" Revin gasped.

"I keep each of my arm braces loaded with a poisoned dart," he said. "They must have figured me for no threat. But they were wrong.

"But that coachman?" the Professor continued. "How did you end up choosing him?"

"His name was first on the list: Arthur Aaron," Revin replied.

The Professor stared at Revin, his expression unreadable.

"Revin," said the Professor. "Come over here for a moment."

Revin approached.

"Now lean over a bit," the Professor instructed him.

Revin leaned over bringing his head closer.

The professor slapped him with parental affection on the side of his head.

"Ow!"

"You bonehead!" the Professor said. "Don't ever pick the first of anything — especially with a name like 'Aaron' that was probably contrived to appear at the top of the list. Sheesh!"

Revin blushed, abashed.

"It also explains why earlier he was so eager to push on," the Professor said. "He needed to get here to carry out the ambush.

"His confederates must have gotten here ahead of us, somehow," the Professor said. "Look around, longshanks. There aren't any other trees nearby. But do you see any relief that might be enough to conceal a couple of horses? Scout around a little. But be cautious in case there are any more."

Revin was glad to be alone with his thoughts for a few minutes because he was so embarrassed about his lack of judgment. "How could I have been so stupid?" Revin thought. He shuddered to think how close they had just come to a bad end.

After a few minutes of circling around the campsite, Revin spotted a little dip of the land and, sure enough, he found two horses staked out in it. Revin pulled up the stakes and led the horses back to their campsite. Then he made a second trip to collect their saddles and tack.

The Professor had not been idle during Revin's absence. Using a rope, he had tied one end to two of the bodies in turn, hand-walked a ways into the grass, then dragged the body away. He tied Art's body last, but he left it to Revin to drag his body away.

"I'm really sorry," Revin said. "It's all my fault that ..."

"Do you want me to slap you again?" the Professor barked.

Revin paused, wild-eyed.

"It's not your fault," the Professor continued. "It's their fault for attacking us. You might have been foolish. But everyone is foolish until they learn better. And you've learned, haven't you?"

"Yes," Revin said sincerely. "I won't make that mistake again."

"Good enough. Now take this!" the Professor said, handing him two coins. "They didn't have much money. But Art had two reggies, and they each had one. So that's four: two for you and two for me."

"That must be the earnest money I had paid," Revin said.

With that, they retired to their bedrolls.

Revin watched the stars overhead for a few minutes. They looked spectacular so far from human habitation. He fell asleep to the chorus of crickets and other night insects.

• • •

In the morning, Revin tried to hook up the horses to the coach and discovered he had absolutely no idea what he was doing. He had never worked with horses before. There had been some ponies in the mines in his town growing up, but he had never done more than ride on one, once, as a child, at a fair.

He tried to fake his way through it and managed to get the tacking on. The horses weren't happy, though. Moreover, they seemed to be able to tell he was nervous and one gave him a painful nip. They also evidently had particular places they wanted to be in the team and were quite nasty about Revin getting it wrong.

As Revin brought the next horse to the coach, it tried to kick him. He partially dodged, but a glancing blow still caught him in the solar plexus and knocked the wind out of him.

Revin sat on the ground, gasping. He was coming to despise horses.

"Are you alright?" the Professor asked from inside the coach.

"No," Revin growled. "These horses are going to be the death of me."

The Professor chuckled as Revin got back to his feet, brushed himself off, and got back to getting the team hooked up.

Eventually, after they were all in their traces, Revin tied up the other two horses to the rear of the coach. Then he climbed onto the box, released the brake, shook the reins, and clicked his tongue as he'd heard the coachman do. The horses shuffled a bit, but did nothing. Revin growled and picked up the coach-whip and only then did the horses begin to walk and, with a bit more encouragement by snapping the reins, he got them to trot.

After perhaps an hour, Revin noticed that the horses were not in sync and kept shying to the right. He slowed down near a farm, trying to figure out what the problem was. A young woman, pulling weeds in the garden, looked up as they went by. Revin tried to guess her age, but she was skinny — almost malnourished, Revin thought — which made her age hard to ascertain. She was barefoot, wearing a grubby shift, and wore a leather collar around her neck like a dog.

"You have the harness hooked up wrong, mister," she said.

"Here, now, missy," the foreman said. "What have I told you about talking to passers-by."

"No, boss," she said, with a terrified expression. "Please don't!"

The foreman pulled out the switch he had tucked in his belt and started to thrash the girl, who lay in the dirt sobbing.

Revin set the brake, checked that he had his sword, and jumped down from the box.

"Hold on," he said.

"Mind your own business, mister," the foreman said. "Unless you want to buy this worthless thing."

"Buy?" Revin asked, aghast.

"She owes 2 reggies," he said. "And until she pays it off, she works for me."

Revin reached into his pocket and pulled out the 2 reggies he had gotten the night before.

"Here," he said.

"What?" the man said, stunned.

"Here. Take the money. She's mine now."

"Now, wait just a minute," the foreman said, beginning to recover his aplomb.

Revin fixed the man with a glare, started to reach for his sword, then realized he still had the coachwhip hanging from his wrist on its cord. He grasped it and menaced the foreman with one hand while still holding out the coins in the other.

"Here's your money!" he snapped. "Let her go."

"Fine!" he snarled, snatching the coins. "Good riddance. She's your problem now."

Revin crouched next to the girl and extended a hand. She cautiously accepted it and Revin helped her to her feet.

"My name is Revin," he said. "What's yours?"

"Lidja, Milord," she replied. "Are you my boss now? Are you going to use that on me?"

"What? No!" Revin said, releasing the whip so it hung again from the cord around his wrist. "No. That was for these stupid horses."

"Horses aren't stupid," she said. "You just have to know how to talk to them."

"Well, would you talk to them for us?" Revin asked simply.

She looked at him uncomprehendingly at first, then her eyes got bigger as she started to dare to hope.

"Really?" she asked.

"Really," Revin said. "Now let's get that collar off."

"But I have to wear the collar until my indenture is done," she said.

Revin loosened the collar and removed it from her neck.

"There," he said. "Done. Complete. Finished. Over."

She stood motionless, speechless. Then tears started to fall. Revin wished he had a handkerchief or something to give her.

"You're free now," Revin said. "That means, you don't have to come with us. And I will understand if you choose not to: You don't know us at all. But if you're willing to take care of our horses and drive the coach, I'll pay you the same as we were paying our previous coachman."

She nodded and walked over to the horses, still crying freely. She went up to each horse, rubbed its nose, and whispered to it too quietly for Revin to hear. Then, when she had recovered her composure, she adjusted and reconnected the harnesses and joined Revin on the box.

She lifted the reins lightly and shook them once. The horses immediately started trotting and fell into a comfortable rhythm. Revin leaned back with a smile, looked up at the sky, and then closed his eyes. Things were looking up.

Then he heard her stomach growl.

"Are you hungry?" he asked.

"I'm fine, Milord" she said. "You don't need to go to any trouble."

"Hey, Professor," he called into the window into the coach. "Pass me some of that jerky."

"Good!" he said handing it up. "You could use some more flesh on those bones."

"It's not for me!" Revin said, scandalized, over the Professor's chuckle.

He accepted the jerky and handed it over to Lidja. "Here's something to tide you over until lunch."

She accepted it and took a bite and then another and another.

Revin called down again, "Pass up that canteen too."

She took the canteen, still chewing, swallowed, and then drank deeply.

"Why are you being so nice to me, Milord?" she said. "You're scaring me that something bad is going to happen."

"First of all, you don't need to call me 'milord'," Revin said. "Just call me Revin. And you can just call my uncle back there 'Professor'.

"Second, I don't think I'm being so nice. You're performing an important service for us for which you will be compensated. I'm sorry you've had such a rough time up until now that being treated like a regular person seems so unusual."

"I'm going to cry again, Mil… Revin," she said, snuffling.

"Well, stop the coach for a minute," Revin said.

Lidja brought the horses to a stop. Revin set the brake.

He climbed down, went to his trunk, and fished around until he found a clean handkerchief. He climbed back up and handed it to her.

"Here," he said. "Cry all you want."

She started the horses again, but then said, "Now you're making me cry and laugh at the same time and it kinda hurts."

They both laughed together.

In the mid-afternoon, they arrived at the town of Relsington, which was at the foot of the hill where the Hermitage was located. They stopped in town primarily so Lidja could purchase some things. Revin paid her the equivalent of 4 reggies as earnest money: three as gold coins and the last as 10 silver miners, so she could avoid attracting notice by spending gold.

Lidja checked the supplies for the horses. With the two additional horses, there was insufficient fodder, so she purchased more, a peck of apples, and some carrots. She gave each of the horses an apple and then went to a clothing store. When she emerged, she was wearing some kind of simple uniform with a white shirt and black trousers.

"I think these are for servants at the Hermitage," she said. "But they were inexpensive, they fit, and I thought they made me look official."

Revin nodded, pleased that she was stepping into her role so effectively.

•　　•　　•

They arrived at the Hermitage, a sprawling complex of buildings at the top of a large hill, in the late afternoon. The tourist map had described it as the first scholarly community in Havelock. It was created when a noble deeded his estate and expansive library to support research and advanced academic study. According to the map, the scholars claimed that the isolation fostered novel research and innovation.

A guard received Revin and the Professor and directed them to check in with the office. He also told Lidja to take the coach to the stables to bed down the horses. She could eat and bunk with the servants, he said.

"Will you be okay?" Revin asked.

"I'm sure I will be fine," she said. "This has to be easier than how I was living before."

Revin waved Lidja on and then walked with the Professor to check in at the office.

He passed the note from the Seneschal to the man at the reception desk and was soon escorted in to meet the Director. He was a tall, cadaverously thin, elderly man who spoke with an odd accent.

"Thank you for coming," he said, putting down the note and standing. "I am Director Solzen. We serve at the pleasure of the Duke."

"Thank you for assisting with my mission," Revin said. "I am Revin Minerson and this is my ... uh ... uncle."

"Professor Grexin! It's an honor to meet you again! Aren't you retired? I read your recent note on etheric wave theory. It's amazing how you keep going."

"Solzen, eh?" the Professor said. "Hmm. We must have met when I was still at the Royal Academy on Harway."

"That's right," he said. "I attended a conference there and you were the featured speaker. While you're here, let me give you both a short tour. And then I'll introduce you to Kief Senterson, the young man you'll be taking to Beskin Harbor."

The Director took them first to the library that was the pride of the institution. It was stupendous. A few weeks ago, Revin would have been awestruck. But honestly, it paled in comparison to the Belthingstone library he had just visited. Still, he was careful to express his thorough appreciation.

Afterward, the Director led them on visits to several of the labs and research spaces, including agricultural, medical, and geological research groups. At each lab, students and researchers recognized the Professor, asking him pointed and insightful questions. Finally, they headed to a newer building nearby.

"Welcome to our new Etheric Studies Building!" Director Solzen said with a flourish. "We have the leading group studying etheric phenomena of all kinds here. And let me introduce Professor Kief Senterson."

Kief, a young man in his late 20s or early 30s. Tall, slim, and bearded, with a slightly hooked nose, he gave them a warm smile.

"Senterson ..." the Professor mused. "You're not related to Baxter Senterson, are you?"

"My father," he said. "You must be Professor Grexin. My father spoke highly of you when you worked together in the Royal Academy."

"Bullshit," the Professor said. "We hated each other."

"He had a lot of respect for you, nonetheless," Kief said. "But, politically, you were far apart, I think."

After introductions, Kief walked them through the building and showed some of the work they were doing, although several of the doors were closed with signs indicating that they were off-limits to unauthorized personnel.

"Shall we dine together?" the Director said after the tour.

"May we have a few minutes to freshen up?" Revin asked. "I also want to check on our driver."

"Surely," the Director said. "We have rooms for you. My assistant can get your keys. We'll meet in the private dining room at six bells."

After getting to his room, and washing his face with the bowl and pitcher of water provided, Revin ran down to the servant's quarters to check on Lidja. He peeked in the dining room and saw her seated among a raucous crowd of cheerful people, laughing and seemingly at ease. He smiled to himself and slipped away without interrupting.

He arrived at the private dining room as the others were filing in, seating themselves around a large table with candles and elaborate place settings. A team of solemn servants stood back from the table as the Director and senior faculty arrived. After everyone was seated, the servants went around the table pouring wine. Once everyone had been served, one of the younger faculty, seated to the right of the Director, stood up.

"I would like to propose a toast," he said, raising his glass. "To our most excellent colleague, Kief Senterson, who goes now, for the confusion of our enemy, to complete his great work of science and engineering. May it tip the balance in this terrible war and rain utter destruction upon the bestial foe!"

"Hear, hear!" several of those gathered said.

Revin felt like he was going to be sick.

The Professor said nothing, but he poured his wine out on the floor. "Excuse me," he said. He slipped out of his seat, dropped to the floor, and hand-walked out of the room.

"What's his problem?" someone said.

"He's always been like that," Kief said. "At least, according to my father. He is on record saying that war is always wrong and that scientists should refuse to allow their work to be co-opted by the nobility."

"What do you think, Revin?" asked the Director.

Everyone turned and looked at Revin.

Revin cleared his throat uncomfortably. "I am here as the representative of the Duke," Revin said. "My own feelings on the matter are immaterial as I have accepted this charge and will carry it out to the best of my ability."

"Well spoken," the Director said, as others nodded. "A very diplomatic non-answer. I perceive you will have a successful career in politics."

"Hear, hear," Revin said, lifting his glass to chuckles all around.

With the toast out of the way, Revin was concerned that his lack of knowledge about polite dining would make him stand out. But he needn't have worried. The scientists couldn't care less about etiquette and appeared to use forks and spoons randomly — or not at all — which allowed Revin to relax and enjoy the meal. Watching the servants, though, he began to awaken to how easy it was to become complacent about your station in life. And to become complicit in sustaining inequalities. His respect for the Professor went up, to be willing to be true to himself and publicly demonstrate his commitment to his principles. And he began to see how the Professor and Will, a captain of pirates, had found common ground.

The meal had five courses: an appetizer of delicately seasoned quail's eggs; a salad with a light, creamy dressing; a main course with tender medallions of beef, spring vegetables, and buttered potatoes; a cheesecake for dessert, drizzled with a raspberry syrup; and, finally, some small candies served with a syrupy, highly aromatic digestif. Revin finally pushed back from the table uncomfortably full and returned to his room for the night.

Too full to sleep, Revin pulled out Momo's journal and began to write. He was careful not to put anything incriminating in writing, but instead offered a carefully redacted history of the events, lingering over the natural beauty of his trip by coach, the despicable behavior of horses, and the sumptuous repast he'd just enjoyed. He found himself avoiding any mention of Lidja and he wondered why. Was he avoiding making her worry about his fidelity? Did he have any right to expect her to feel jealous? Was he presumptuous to even imagine considering Lidja in romantic terms?

Finally, he set the journal aside and put himself — and his questions — to bed.

•　　　•　　　•

The next morning, the man in the office directed Revin to the cafeteria for a light breakfast, where he met with the Professor chatting with the Director. Kief arrived a few minutes later. Revin barely listened while they discussed the nature of etheric phenomena and whether they were more like one thing or another — the whole conversation was over his head.

"Your coach should be ready by now," the Director said. "I asked them to have it here by the end of breakfast. Oh! And I had them pack you a picnic lunch to enjoy enroute. Travel well!"

Revin carried their bags out to the driveway and found Lidja standing at attention next to the door to the coach. She held the door for the Professor while Revin stowed their gear in the storage compartment. A few moments later, Kief came out with a bag for Revin to stow in the back and a separate document case he kept with himself.

"Let me caution you," he said to everyone. "This case has a small incendiary charge in it that will destroy the secret documents inside if the case is tampered with. I'm telling you this, and keeping it with me, in case it goes off when we go over a bump or something, in which case one of us should endeavor to throw it out before it sets the coach on fire."

With that, Revin shut the coach door and climbed up on the box with Lidja. She gently shook the reins and the horses trotted off. Revin consulted their map and helped Lidja find the right turn in Relsington to head West toward Sendia Springs and then to Beskin Harbor.

It was a beautiful day with sun and just a few puffy, white clouds. Revin chatted amiably with Lidja, who appeared in high spirits. Revin snuck glances at her beaming with rosy cheeks. She recounted how much fun she'd had with the lively community of staff at the Hermitage.

The morning passed quickly. Around noon, they stopped to have the lunch the Director had arranged for them. Lidja watered the horses and gave them some fodder, then joined the three men for lunch.

After lunch, they were making preparations to depart and Revin considered sitting in the coach for a bit, but he found the technical conversations between the Professor and other scholars so far over his head that it tended to be extremely tedious. He shook his head and rejoined Lidja on the box as she started the horses.

In the early afternoon, they passed over a series of rolling hills. Revin manned the brake on the descents to keep the coach from rolling over the horses. On the highest hill, they paused to look out over the surrounding territory. The grassland, probably connected to where they had stayed the first night, seemed to extend to the horizons.

By mid-afternoon, Revin spotted clouds of steam rising in the distance and, a half-hour later, they arrived at Sendia Springs.

The inn was a large wooden building with a red tile roof that had a stable and several outbuildings next to a steaming river that flowed along the face of a set of low terraces — some white, some colored a brownish-yellow, and some gray. Steaming water trickled over the colored terraces and running down into a braided stream that passed in front of the hotel. Revin sat awestruck by the natural beauty. He snuck a glance at Lidja to see that she too was speechless with wonder and fascination.

Lidja forded the coach across the streams and around to the front of the hotel. A porter ran to collect their bags and show them inside. Several men from the stables came over to take charge of the coach and horses. At first, Lidja was reluctant to let the horses go without her, but Revin persuaded her to come with them into the lobby.

A woman wearing traditional dress, greeted them just inside the door.

"Greetings, honored travelers," she said bowing low. "Welcome to Sendia Springs, the premier resort on the Island of Havelock. We're very glad you are here and we hope you will let us see to your every desire. How many are you?"

"There are four of us," Revin said.

"How many rooms do you require?" the hostess asked.

"Well, um ..." Revin started.

"We can share a room, can't we, Professor?" said Kief.

"Surely," the Professor agreed.

"So ..." Revin fumbled for words.

"If you please, Revin," Lidja said. "May I share a room with you? If ... that's alright ..."

"Well ..." Revin began, reluctant to give up his privacy. But then he saw her face so full of hope, yet worried that he would say no. "Yes! Yes, of course, I'll share a room with you."

"Yay!" she said.

The hostess gave them their keys and led them to two adjoining rooms. She pointed out the features of the rooms and showed them where there were robes and towels for the bathing facilities and hot springs. Then she bowed deeply again and bade them welcome one last time.

After everyone had freshened up and changed into robes, they went to the dining room for dinner. They were seated at a low table and served by an impeccable wait staff that brought course after course of small plates for them to sample. The first plates held pickled vegetables and mushrooms that were both sour and salty. Next came fish eggs and crackers, reminding

Revin of his last fateful meal aboard the *Madeline*. His eyes kept being drawn back to Lidja, who had never experienced anything like this before. Her eyes sparkled as she sampled the different dishes; she squealed with excitement when the waiter drenched a block of cheese with spirits, lit it on fire, and then extinguished the flames with the juice of a lime.

"Revin?" the Professor said. "Revin!"

"Huh?" Revin said. He noticed that Kief had stepped away from the table.

"After dinner, perhaps you can take our guest to the hot springs. I think I'll turn in early — if you know what I mean."

"Huh?" Revin said, now totally confused.

The Professor rolled his eyes.

"Revin!" the Professor said sternly. "Do you remember why we came on this little jaunt? This might be our best chance."

"Oh, right! So I just need to ..." Revin said and then realized what he was saying. "Wait! How am I going to take him to the hot spring?"

Revin, who had been walking on clouds all evening, was suddenly dragged back down to earth. He wracked his brain trying to come up with some plan or excuse or something. The springs were gendered and he fully recognized that he would be unable to pass, naked, in the men's bath. He began to sweat as he tried to think of something. Anything. He looked up uncomfortably when Kief returned to the table with another man standing behind him.

"Hey," Kief said, a little nervously, looking down. "So I ran into an ... old friend that I haven't seen for a really long time. I don't mean to cut out on you, but I want to catch up with him tonight. So, if you don't mind, I think he and I will visit the baths and then spend the evening together."

"So don't wait up for you, is what you're saying?" asked the Professor with a wink.

"Yes," Kief said, looking up with a relieved laugh. "Yes, exactly."

After dinner, Revin walked back to their rooms with the Professor and Lidja.

"Have fun, kids," the Professor said, yawning. "I'll see you in the morning."

"Good night ... Uncle," Revin said.

Revin unlocked the door and held it for Lidja.

"Are you ready to go to the hot spring?" she asked.

"Well ... Um ..." Revin said. "To be honest, that's kind of complicated for me."

"Is it because you're actually a girl?" she asked. The blood drained out of Revin's face.

"What?" Revin squeaked, backing up against the wall. "How did ..."

"I don't know," she said. "It wasn't any one thing. But I figured it out last night when you came to check on me. I saw you there at the door and something ... just clicked for me."

"I mean, I'm not a girl," Revin said. "I realized that a long time ago. But I still look like this."

"So I understand that you can't go to the men's bath," Lidja said. "But why not come to the women's side anyway. There won't be anyone you know there."

She approached Revin and took his hand in hers.

"Please," she said. "For me?"

Revin knew these feelings weren't right. There were so many things wrong with it morally and ethically — not the least of which was his relationship with her as both rescuer and employer. But he just couldn't bring himself to say no.

He removed his chest binding and undid his hair. They both took their towels and, after Revin closed the door, he let her take his hand as they walked together to the hot springs.

Inside was a steam-filled room with piping that had hot water sprinkling at many stations throughout the room. They seemed to be the only ones there.

They disrobed and Lidja pulled him to one of the showers.

"Let me wash you," she said. "Then you can wash me."

He stood under the deliciously hot spray while she shampooed his hair and the rest of his body.

After he'd rinsed, she handed him the shampoo and turned her back. He began to wash her hair. It was a strange feeling to be so intimate with another person — terrifying, yet amazingly satisfying.

"Your poor hair is so short," he said. "And so ragged."

"I had to cut it myself. It was easier, that way," she said. "Then they couldn't pull it."

Revin suddenly choked up and began fighting back tears.

"I can't believe someone did that to you," he said, hoarsely. "I can't believe people can do that to one another."

"Thank you, Revin," she said, tilting her head back and smiling up at him. "For caring."

He moved on to the rest of her body. He could feel her shoulder blades and ribs. And he could see the sharp lines of her pelvis.

"Did they starve you too?" he asked.

"We never had enough to eat," she said. "I was always hungry."

"How long were you there?" Revin asked.

"Let's see," she said. "I was sent there when I was thirteen so ... four years."

"Wait!" Revin said, shocked. "You're as old as I am! I thought you were a lot younger."

"Well, I'm not," she said, turning around, so they stood face to face. She looked up, meeting his eyes.

Revin blushed all the way to the floor.

"Let's ... Let's go into the hot spring now," he whispered.

They walked into the next room. They found a large, irregularly shaped pool filled with steaming water that gave off a strong smell of sulfur. They dipped their toes into it, looking for a place where the temperature was right, and then slipped into the pool.

Revin found a place where they could sit and look east. It was well after dark, but he could see the stars rising above the distant hills they'd traveled over earlier in the day. The braided stream below them sparkled with starlight. The rising steam looked like ghosts in the darkness. Lidja sat down next to Revin and then edged herself up against him.

"Revin," she said. "I think ... I think I love you."

"Lidja, I ... I ... "

"Is there someone else?" she asked.

"No," Revin said, nodding. "Wait! Yes? Maybe? I don't know. I'm so confused."

She wrapped her arms around him.

"Then let's not think about that tonight and just have a nice time."

Revin, initially tense, relaxed after a moment and leaned his head over onto her head and they sat contentedly together in the dark for a long while.

Eventually, they began to get too hot, so they climbed up and sat on the edge of the pool with just their legs in the water.

"How did you come to know so much about horses?" Revin asked.

"When I was a little girl, we had horses on our farm," she began. Revin was charmed, listening to her monologue about her fascination with horses. He smiled in the dark as she nattered on excitedly.

Finally, they reluctantly pulled their feet out of the pool, put their robes back on, and returned to their room.

As soon as they entered, Revin heard tapping at the adjoining door. He opened it to witness the Professor doing a double-take at seeing Revin with his hair down and without his chest binding. Then he quickly started whispering.

"Get in here," the Professor hissed. "I need your help!"

"I'll be back in a bit, Lidja," Revin said and stepped through the doorway.

"What do you need?"

"Grab a pen and start copying!" the Professor whispered.

Revin spied a thick sheaf of pages with dense writing on them. The Professor had already copied many of the pages, but there were many more to go. Revin picked up a pen and a clean sheet of paper and got to work.

Every few pages, Revin remembered Lidja in the next room. He hoped she was sleeping and wasn't worrying about him. He sighed, knuckled down, and got back to work copying.

Four hours later, in the early hours of the morning, they wrapped up. The Professor stowed their copies in his trunk and returned the pages to Kief's document case and carefully closed it.

"Get ready ... Here goes nothing," he said, and pulled a long strip of paper out through the closed and locked top. Nothing happened.

"Ha! I think I got the boobytrap re-enabled," he said. "It took me a long time to figure that out."

"I can't believe we managed to copy the whole thing," Revin said, flexing his fingers. "I haven't written so much in months."

"Off to bed with you now, young man," the Professor said. "We've got one more long day before us, but then I think we'll be on our way home."

Revin crept back through the adjoining door. He started to climb into his own bed when Lidja spoke.

"Could you come over here, Revin?" she said, quietly. "To keep me company? I keep worrying that I'll wake up and this will all have been a dream."

Revin hesitated for a moment. He recognized if he did this, he was crossing a line from which there was no return, but he couldn't bring himself to stop. He laid his robe on the other bed and then slipped into bed with her. She snuggled up against him and kissed his cheek. He turned toward her and she pressed her mouth to his. Fireworks went off in Revin's head as he slid his arms around her and desperately kissed her back.

•   •   •

In the morning, Revin awoke and was surprised to find himself alone in the bed. He got up, dressed, and then sat and wrote a couple of letters. He also counted out four reggies. He was about to go to breakfast when Lidja returned.

"Where were you?" Revin asked.

"Just checking on the horses," she said. "They're good here, but it never hurts for them to know you're watching. Oh! Someone asked about those two spare horses and whether we'd like to sell them."

"Sure," Revin said. "In a minute you can go do that, if you like. But first, I need to say something that may change your mind."

Lidja looked worried, so he took her hand.

"When we get to Beskin Harbor to drop off Kief, the Professor and I will be departing as well," Revin said. "So I want to pay you the rest of the money you're owed. And I'd like you to deliver these two letters for me. One is to Mr. Darkpony, who rented us the coach. There is a deposit on the coach and, when you return it, you can keep that as well. That should be enough money to set yourself up for a good little while. But if the horses would suit you better than money, you could keep them."

"No," she said. "A horse is a lot of expense, unless you need it for something in particular. So I think selling them is the right thing to do. But is it really okay for me to keep the money?"

"You keep it," Revin said, and then continued. "The other letter is to the Duke's seneschal. He's expecting me to come back to the capital. This letter says I've completed the task he set me, but that I have some family business to attend to and won't be back for a while. It also includes an introduction to you which perhaps might lead to something. Can you deliver these for me?"

"I will," she said. "But … Where are you going? When will I see you again?"

"I'm … Actually, I'm here in disguise because … I'm a p-pirate," Revin said, stumbling over the word. "I don't know when I'll be able to come back. But! But if you write to me on Candlemain, I should be able to get it. And so you can tell me where you go so I can find you and see you again. If … If you want to see me again."

"Oh, Revin," she said, hugging him. "Of course I want to see you again. I want to see you always. I love you so much that I can't bear we're going to be apart. But I will understand and respect whatever your heart chooses."

Revin was struck by Lidja's certainty — and courage. His feelings were such a tangle, he could barely bring himself to meet her gaze. He gave her the letters and the money. While Lidja went to sell the spare horses, Revin checked on the Professor.

After packing, the three of them went to breakfast where they found Kief already there with his "old friend".

After a hearty breakfast, the four emerged to find the bags already loaded, the coach freshly washed and shined, with the horses brushed and combed and little red ribbons tied in their manes. While Revin paid the hefty bill with the last of the Seneschal's money, The Professor and Kief seated themselves in the coach while Lidja walked to each of the horses, as she did every time, to rub their noses and whisper little words of encouragement.

Then they set out on the last leg of their journey.

•   •   •

By late afternoon, the horses were tired, but they were nearly to Beskin Harbor, so they pushed on. Revin had divided his time this day between sitting on the box with Lidja and sitting in the coach with Kief and the Professor, although he still found their dialog tedious in larger doses. The Professor was asking about the dynamics of etheric stream formation and the role atmospheric conditions played. As best as Revin could understand, Kief was arguing that atmospheric conditions played only a mediating influence -- whatever that meant. But the Professor grasped the significance immediately and followed up with yet another, deeper question. Revin rolled his eyes, and leaned back to nap for a bit until they arrived.

Revin awoke when the coach came to a stop. It was now dark. Revin looked out and could see the pier at Beskin Harbor with peaceful waves lapping on the shore. He stretched, then got up and opened the door.

"I believe this is where you get off," he said to Kief.

"Yes," he said. "We're working with the boat at the end of the pier, there."

Revin climbed out and held the door. Kief stepped out onto the running board.

A bright light suddenly appeared in the sky over Beskin Harbor — some kind of firework? — and Revin could hear the sounds of yelling and screaming coming from the end of the pier.

"It's a raid," the Professor said, looking through the window. "Those are marines — probably from Belleriand. We should pull back."

"What are they doing?" Kief asked.

"We're not waiting to find out," Revin said, pushing Kief back into the coach and climbing up onto the box. "Lidja! Get us out of here!"

Lidja shook the reins and the horses started up. A party of marines racing to secure the end of the pier spotted the coach. They charged out and two of them caught hold of the coach, climbing up on the footboards at the back. Revin threw himself onto the roof of the coach and slithered on his belly toward the back.

The hands of one of the marines appeared and grabbed the bars around the top of the roof. Revin grabbed his sword and clumsily struck out at the hands. The unseen man yelled as he lost his grip and fell off the footboard. Suddenly, a towline appeared, stabbing up into the sky momentarily, and the other soldier sprang up on the towline and landed on the roof. He stamped his foot down on Revin's sword and stood over him with his own sword drawn.

"Stop the coach!" the soldier called to Lidja. "Stop! Or he dies!"

Lidja cracked the whip and the horses bolted forward. The man drew back his arm to strike, then the carriage suddenly passed under the low archway that led into the promenade and the soldier was swept off the top of the carriage.

Lidja kept the horses at a gallop until they turned the corner at the end of the promenade and entered a plaza. Then she reined in the horses to a walk.

She looked back toward Revin."Orders?"

Revin surveyed the situation under the fading light of the pyrotechnic. A building stood between them and the harbor, but he could hear the continued sounds of combat. He could make out people running for buildings to get under cover. Another pyrotechnic went up and Revin suddenly spotted towlines and then an airship.

It was the *Queen*, Revin realized! She had come to investigate the activity.

"The Professor and I will disembark here," Revin said. "You and Kief should put as much distance between yourselves and the marines as possible. They would love nothing more than to capture or kill him. Head south to the capital."

"What are you going to do, Revin?" Lidja asked, her voice breaking with worry.

"I have a plan."

Revin pulled out his signaling mirror and began trying to get the attention of the *Queen*. Revin wasn't sure the flares were bright enough, but they were evidently watching carefully and, after several moments, he saw the countersign and the *Queen* began to descend into the plaza.

Revin grabbed their trunks that contained the all-important copy of the plans, and dragged them out of the carriage.

"Go!" he yelled to Lidja.

The coach rolled away.

The *Queen* touched down and the Professor hurried aboard with his arm braces while two teams of pirates ran out to collect their trunks. Revin started to run, but an inexorable force grabbed him and slammed him back against the wall of the building. The remmer marine had climbed on top of the building and had made a towline, pinning Revin to the wall.

"Go!" Revin cried to the *Queen*.

Two more airships appeared in the sky over Beskin Harbor as Revin struggled to free himself. He saw Will at the gangplank looking around and then spotting him.

"Look out!" Revin screamed. "It's a trick!"

Whatever might have happened next was preempted when a brilliant white flash illuminated the clouds from below. A ring of blue coruscating lightning bolts reached up toward the sky and began to whirl around an axis faster and faster. Revin realized the Etheric Storm Generator must have been triggered.

Suddenly, Revin felt the force holding him back vanish. All of the towlines had vanished. He sprinted for the *Queen* as she began to rise without towlines to hold her down. He leapt and caught the end of the gangplank with one hand, leaving him dangling as the craft rose higher and higher.

Will calmly walked straight out to the very end, reached down, caught Revin's hand, and pulled him up.

"Welcome home, lad," he said, with a grin, giving Revin a hug. "I somehow knew you'd be at the heart of all this."

The wind was already rising by the time they reached the cockpit. Will headed straight back to the remmer deck. The *Queen* began to vibrate and slip to the west as, without remmers to hold her on course, the wind began to drag her back into the storm.

"No streams, Will!" Grip said. "They can't see a single stream."

"Call life lines," Will said. "This is going to be a rough one."

"Attach life lines!" Grip called fore and aft. "Attach life lines!"

Will got out his monocle and began searching high and low.

A long pause followed while everyone simply watched him.

"There!" he called. "Down! Due east! Inland!"

He bound a towline no thicker than yarn. The others began trying and, after a few moments, the *Queen* stopped losing ground and began to move sluggishly east.

Revin went to the observation deck and watched as the storm grew before his eyes. The other two airships had lost all their attachments and were being pulled rapidly into the storm. In moments, they were lost to view in the nearly constant flashes of lightning one on top of another. He already couldn't see the town through the blinding sheets of rain. He could see two funnel clouds circulating around the center of the storm over the harbor. Buildings were torn apart and the air was filled with debris.

The *Queen* continued to bounce up and down with the turbulence, even as she crept away from the storm that only grew in magnitude behind her. Revin watched in horror as the town was engulfed and flattened by the storm. He couldn't imagine there would be anything left but rubble by morning.

He looked down and spotted the coach headed south toward the capital. But as they crept away from the storm and could reach more etheric streams, the *Queen of Belleriand* turned north and the coach was lost from Revin's view.

ABOUT THE AUTHOR

Steven D. Brewer has been a fan of science fiction and fantasy stories for as long as he can remember. He still remembers getting scolded for not reading chapter books in fourth grade because he was avidly consuming *The Hobbit* late at night, by flashlight under his covers. And he probably got his copy from his older brother and most important mentor.

Steven currently teaches scientific writing at the University of Massachusetts Amherst. He lives in Amherst, Massachusetts with his extended family.

ALSO IN THIS SERIES

THE THIRD TIME'S THE CHARM

BOOK ONE OF *REVIN'S HEART*

When an airship is hijacked by pirates, a young man with a secret loses his mentor ... and his future.

FOR THE FAVOR OF A LADY

BOOK TWO OF *REVIN'S HEART*

Even a pirate will stop at nothing to help his little sister.

STORM CLOUDS GATHER

BOOK THREE OF *REVIN'S HEART*

After the Queen of Belleriand encounters an etheric anomaly that threatens the airship, Revin is abducted. But by whom? And why?

Available in digital and trade paperback editions from
Water Dragon Publishing
waterdragonpublishing.com

YOU MIGHT ALSO ENJOY

THE ALCHEMIST DAUGHTER
by Paul S. Moore

When a concoction of ethers channels a little of their magic properties to one location, inspiration springs to life.

GREY MOTHER MOUNTAIN
by Elyse Russell

When her village is destroyed, an elderly woman seeks help from the last remaining dragon to get revenge.

SONGS OF A DEAD FOREST
by Travis Wade Beaty

Old songs can bring new life.

Available in digital and trade paperback editions from
Water Dragon Publishing
waterdragonpublishing.com

www.ingramcontent.com/pod-product-compliance
Lightning Source LLC
Chambersburg PA
CBHW051302190726
48286CB00004B/1215